the Antics of Reggie and the Exotic Bird Haven

Kimberly Hughey

illustrated by
Elena Kochetova

Text and Illustrations copyright © 2020 Kimberly Hughey

Published by Amazing Books Press
For orders, please contact: **amazingbooks343@gmail.com**

Cover Design and Illustrations by Elena Kochetova
lalyla489@gmail.com

Hardback ISBN-13: 978-1-7333891-7-4
Paperback ISBN-13:978- 1-7333891-8-1
eBook ISBN- 13: 978-1-7333891-9-8

Library of Congress Control Number:
TBD

Hughey, Kimberly

The Antics of Reggie and The Exotic Bird Haven / Kimberly Hughey

The Antics of Reggie and The Exotic Bird Haven takes you on a journey with Reggie where he thinks being an exotic bird will give him a better life. But he soon finds out what it's really like to be a bird he is not meant to be. What challenges will face? What will he learn along the way from the choices he made? Take a peek inside to find out!

This book is dedicated to those of you who have supported me wholeheartedly throughout my journey as a writer. Your support, encouragement, and kindness mean the world to me because it helps me see each book through to the very end. Everyone's continued love for Reggie encourages me to continue sharing this crazy seagull's comedic antics.

Reggie sat with his friend Goose
on the pilings, yawning with
boredom.

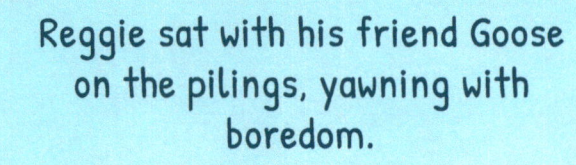

2

"Let's fly to the boardwalk buildings where we haven't been before
to see what goodies we can find there," Reggie suggested.
"Sounds good to me. Let's go!" Goose agreed.

3

As they soared down the boardwalk, they couldn't believe
how colorful and vibrant life was. People were laughing
and relaxing in the warm sun.

4

And there was so much more food to choose from!
Their stomachs rumbled with jealousy from the
restaurants' wonderful smells.

5

Then he saw it...
The most
eye-catching
building of all:
The Exotic
Bird Haven!

"GOOSE,
CHECK
THIS
OUT!"

Reggie said as he stared, in awe of the beautiful birds in the window of the
haven. There was a video playing that showed how carefully they took care
of the exotic birds and the fascinating things they ate.

6

THE EXOTIC BIRD HAVEN

"That's it!"
Reggie shouted with excitement.

"I WANT TO BE AN EXOTIC BIRD!"

Goose was puzzled.
"What? How can you be an exotic bird when you're a seagull? Seagulls are not exotic and never will be. Why would you want to be an exotic bird anyway? Don't you like being you?"

"I do, but didn't you just see the top-notch care exotic birds get? Didn't you see the amazing food they eat? Don't you want that too? Come on, Goose, let's be exotic! We will never have to find our own food again!"

"YOU'RE CRAZY, REG. HOW IN THE WORLD ARE YOU GOING TO BECOME EXOTIC?"

Goose asked, knowing Reggie was going to find a way. "I don't know yet. But I'll figure it out," he said confidently.

"Oh boy. Here we go," Goose mumbled under his breath.

9

Their evening was filled with yummy funnel cakes, fried Oreos, French fries dripping with cheese, and lemonade to wash it all down. "Wow, it got dark quick," Reggie observed. "Let's stay here tonight, Goose." "Sure, I can't wait to see what's for breakfast tomorrow!" Goose smirked.

10

They perched themselves above a house that was having a party, just waiting for their chance to swoop in for some snacks. The smells were something they didn't recognize. Curious, they moved in to get a closer look. Just then, a man came out with something and put it in a big pot, enhancing the smells even more. A bit later, the man came back and pulled the food out of the pot. That's it! Reggie thought. And he began to plan...

11

"Goose, I got it! Did you see the food turning yellow in there? I'm going to take a yellow birdbath and come out a brand new exotic bird!" Reggie exclaimed.

12

"Or a cooked bird!" Goose chuckled. "You're nuts! Don't you see the heat coming off that? Instead of an exotic bird, you'll be a fried bird."
"Oh...yeah, I didn't think about that. I'll just wait 'til it cools down." So Reggie waited and waited, checking it until it was cool enough. Then... He shot up into the air and gleefully fell, diving right into the pot!

13

He dunked himself several times, soaking up all the yellow he could. His splashing made so much noise that people came out to see what was going on.

TIME TO GO!

Reggie squawked to Goose
as they flew to their
perches for the night.
The next morning, Reggie
couldn't wait to go to the Exotic
Bird Haven. He was so excited,
he couldn't even eat breakfast.
Reggie took off and Goose
followed.

The whole way there, Goose tried
to talk Reggie out of it. He knew
this wasn't right and tried to
explain to Reggie all he would be
giving up, but Reggie didn't care.
He was convinced the life of an
exotic bird was better. There was
no talking him out of it.

15

OOH!

AAH!

OOH! OOH!

AAH!

Reggie regally flew down
in front of the haven,
and it didn't take long
for him to get noticed.

The many
"Ooh's!" and "Aah's!"
drew the attention of
the haven. Just like that,
Reggie was taken in, and
his new journey of the
exotic life began.

16

They swooped him up and took him into the back room so they could begin looking him over. They took his measurements, noted his unique color, odd odor, and began their research to find out what type of new exotic bird they were so lucky to find.

"Have you ever seen a bird like this before?" the clerk asked excitedly. "No, and it's beautiful! Did you see the black triangle on his throat? I can just see it now... People will come from all over to see this bird! This is going to be amazing!" the manager exclaimed.

EXOTIC
☑ COLOR
☑ HE...
☑ SIZE
☐ FEATHERS

17

Uh-oh. Something isn't right. Where are all the birds?
And I'm starving. Where is all the exotic food?
Reggie thought as he began to shake with fear.
"Oh, look. The poor thing is shaking. I'm going to put him in his cage
and feed him. What type of food should we give him?" the clerk asked.
The manager responded, "We don't know what type of bird this is yet,
so just give him the fruit and nuts for now."

The clerk tried to get Reggie settled in a 5x5-foot cage,
but Reggie fought with all his might! It was a struggle,
but the clerk was able to gain control and
safely get him in his new home.

18

Reggie was terrified, and also unable to ignore his hunger pains any longer. He couldn't wait for his meal of escargot, and his mouth watered the closer the clerk got with his food.

Finally! I'm starving! He squawked, bending over to take his first bite. As the taste hit his tongue he spit it out instantly in disgust.

YUCK!! WHAT IS THIS?!

he shrieked. Uh, that was gross! he thought. Where is all the exotic food? Where is the escargot and all the amazing food I saw them eating in the video?" he questioned, beginning to panic.

20

21

"That, my friend, is the best bird food in the store! I wish I got that as my meals. I only get seeds," a voice said from the dark corner next to him. "My name's Bean. I'm a red-cheeked cordon bleu. What's your name and what kind of bird are you?" she questioned as she slipped through the bars of her cage and into his.

"My name's Reggie and I'm a seagull." He jumped back, startled by her presence in his space.

22

"SEAGULL?!"

the parakeet next to him screeched. And with that, the other birds chimed in

"I've never seen a yellow seagull before. Were you born that way?" Finnegan, the sun conure, asked innocently.

"What's a seagull doing in here?" asked Bobber, the macaw, nodding his head to the beat of his own question. "Seagulls aren't exotic!" Josie, the sunbird, teased, looking down at him over her long, slim beak.

23

"We all thought you were an exotic bird! Boy, did you have us fooled! You even tricked the owners, and they know their birds," Bean said. Then she turned to the others and yelled,

"QUIET DOWN, BIRDS! LET REGGIE SPEAK!"

24

And they fell silent because
they didn't want to miss his story.
Once Reggie explained how he got there,
they bombarded him with questions.
"I just don't understand why you would
want to give up all the things you had
for this life. You had freedom, Reggie.
We don't have that," Bean said.
"Yeah, you had friends and an amazing
life," Finnegan pointed out.
"And the ability to eat anything you
wanted. You could eat anytime you felt
hungry. Here, we get fed the same thing
day in and day out: 8am and 8pm on the
dot. You'll get used to it."
Bobber nodded.

25

During the quiet hours of the evening, Reggie couldn't stop thinking
about the choice he made. He was beginning to regret it.
Goose was right. He owed him a huge apology if he ever saw him again.
Days went by, and Reggie began to give up, even though
his new friends did their best trying to cheer him up.
Sometimes Bean would make him laugh by playing
"peek-a-boo!" through the open bars.
Some gave him words of encouragement,
while others shared their stories with him,
making him feel better.

26

Since the owners of the store were not able to identify Reggie, they reached out to the public for help. After the Channel 6 News showed up to broadcast the story, Reggie was the talk of the town. People came to the store just to see him, and as they peered at him in his locked cell, he couldn't help but feel very alone in such a crowded place.

NEWS

??? BIRD

27

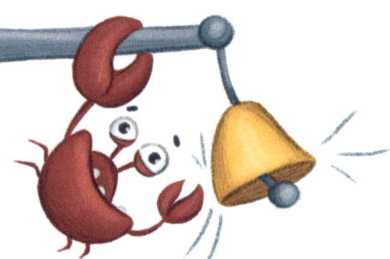

DINNNGG!

the door sounded as another customer entered.
The customer went up to the clerk and said,
"I know that bird, and he's not an exotic bird. That's a
seagull pretending to be exotic. Put this fish sandwich in
front of him and you'll see. Open his cage and watch!"

28

Reggie recognized that familiar voice.
It was Old Man Stan, and instantly, Reggie found hope again!
When the clerk opened his cage, he shot out faster than a cannonball and
barreled right into Old Man Stan. He knew Stan was going to save him from
this place. And he gobbled up that fish sandwich just like Stan said he would!

29

Just then, the door announced the next guest, and in walked another familiar face: the man who made the yellow birdbath for Reggie! The man told the clerk he believed this was the bird that dove into his pot of curry sauce the other night and made a big mess.

The clerk was shocked and immediately got the manager. Yes, he did, indeed, look like a seagull. They could not believe it!

YES!

Reggie thought. I'm going to be free again! Looking around the room, his happiness quickly disappeared. He saw all the gloomy faces of his new friends. They were sad because they knew he was meant to be free and was going to get his wish, which meant they were about to lose a good friend. Reggie flew to the others and said, "Thank you all for being my friend and getting me through this. I will never forget you." They said their good-byes, and Old Man Stan took Reggie outside. From there, the two old friends nodded to each other, and off Reggie went.

31

AHH!

It was great to soar through the air again!
He closed his eyes, basking in the warmth
of the sun and the wind through his
feathers when suddenly...

CRASH!

He collided with another bird that flew into his path.
Reggie plunged into the water while the other bird regained
his flight. When Reggie emerged, he was free of the yellow.
When he looked up, he saw Goose!
"Hey, Reg! Are you okay?
How did being an exotic bird work out?"
Goose asked, excited to see his friend again.

"GOOSE! I am so glad to see you!" he announced.
"I owe you a huge apology. You were right all along. The exotic life is not for me. I love my life...and my friends...and my freedom just the way it is! I will never do that again. I missed being me."
"I'm so glad you're back, Reg! I was really worried about you and really missed my friend," Goose said affectionately.
"It's great to be back, and I can't wait to tell you all about it. Let's grab something to eat. I'm starving," Reggie said.
As they sat and ate their lunch, they caught up on everything they each missed during these last few days. They both had their friend back, and life was back to normal...for now.

the end

33

Thank you so much for reading, "The Antics for Reggie and the Exotic Bird Haven!"
We hope you adored it as much as we enjoyed creating it! If you enjoyed it, please share
a review on Amazon so others will know how much you liked his story!
He would REALLY love to hear your thoughts!
If you want to keep an eye out for the next crazy thing Reggie does, please enter the link
below in your browser. Once you are registered, Reggie will send you a few coloring pages!

https://bit.ly/reggieandtheexoticbirdhaven

See you on the next adventure!

Kimberly Hughey

is passionate about living life to the fullest and has experienced skydiving, flying in a bi-wing plane, tidal bore rafting and white water rafting. When she's not hiking with her family, she is scrapbooking her memories, photographing family and friends, creating jewelry and crafting her next story. She is also the author of, "The Antics of Reggie and Old Man Stan" and "Amazing Holidays: Celebrating Valentine's Day from A-Z."

Elena Kochetova
illustrator

Hi! My name is Elena and I am an illustrator. Like many of us, I look at my childhood through rose-colored glasses. For this reason, my imagination creates cute and funny characters. I love to bring a bit of humor and naivety to the illustrations. I believe that this is the most delicate and correct way to teach and deliver emotions to our readers.

www.ingramcontent.com/pod-product-compliance
Lightning Source LLC
Chambersburg PA
CBHW041546240626
47164CB00003B/145